POOKIE
WANTS OUT!

The Continuing Adventures
of
A HAMSTER's TALE

A Short Story

by

Susan Hauth

POOKIE
WANTS OUT
THE CONTINUING ADVENTURES OF
A HAMSTER's TALE

Published by Susan Hauth Books,

Reno, Nevada

POOKIE
WANTS OUT
THE CONTINUING ADVENTURES OF
A HAMSTER's TALE

Susan Hauth Books, Publishing

ISBN-9781702101042

Illustrations by Tracey Dingess

PRINTED IN THE UNITED STATES OF AMERICA

Dedicated to all Pookies,

past and present.

Acknowledgements

To you Allen, my husband. You are just as much a part of this book as I am. It's your non-stop encouragement and enthusiasm that helps make these stories fun to write. Our combined knowledge and experience with hamsters over the years has given me the necessary insight into their individual personalities and quirky traits to make the stories come alive. Thanks to you, Book #3 is in the works!

And to you Tracey, my sister and illustrator! Once again, you outdid yourself in making each chapter ending have the visual impact I envisioned. You have the talent and insight to take my ideas and make them real. I love the fact that we work so well together, because it makes the many miles between us disappear. I can't thank you enough for giving me your precious time and energy to make this book complete. I am blessed to have you as my sister!

And to you, Tom Gauthier, my editor. The more I work with you, the more I learn. I respect your guidance and experience, and appreciate your patience and advice. The details of putting a book together can be overwhelming, but at any time thru the process, I know I can call on you. I look forward to working with you on my next project. Thank you, Tom!

CHAPTER ONE

Freedom!

Running like I've never run before.

Running through the streets of a tiny town I'd never seen before.

Zipping down Main Street, turning the corner at the candy store onto P-nut Avenue *without even slowing down*!

Then flying past the post office, past the firehouse and the library.

Freedom!

Down Sunnyside Avenue, with its twists and turns as it winds its way through the park, with lush grass and picnic areas on both sides.

It's all a blur as I speed around the fountain, past the playground, around another sharp curve before going into the home stretch!

The home stretch through a field of sunflowers!

Freedom!

Yes, I'm dreaming.

Again.

As I wake up, I realize all of this was real!

It happened!

I relive it often when I sleep.

And it makes me want more.

I can still feel the coolness of the grass in the park when we finished the race.

We were all taken out of our racing balls to relax by the fountain while waiting for the announcement of the winner.

I can still hear the water gently bubbling from the fountain.

And feel the refreshing sprinkles as they splash on my face.

I hear the cheering from the crowd of people gathered around the race track.

Lucy and her parents are applauding and yelling, "Yeah Pookie! You won! You won!"

The other hamsters in the race shake my paw and pat me on my back in congratulations.

Pawsley barks excitedly and brags to the other dogs in the pet store that I am his friend.

I want to experience that feeling again.

Even though I was in my ball for the race and not really *free*, I want to run.

Or climb.

Or race once more.

I want to accomplish *something!*

I want to do some more exploring.

Downstairs.

I'm wide awake now.

And it's time. I climb out of my house like I'd done many times before.

I head straight out the bedroom door to the stairs right across the hall.

I know it's a long way down, and something I've never attempted before.

I'm anxious.

How do I even start?

It's not that I haven't been down there before. But only *safely* in my exercise ball. Usually while Lucy is cleaning my house on Saturdays.

Lucy is the reason I live here.

She's only ten.

But – with her dad's help – she adopted me from the local pet store.

Lucy is why I have a nice house.

Upstairs on her desk.

And the reason I have new friends.

I used to live at the pet store with my Mom and ten siblings.

I look different than all of them.

I'm almost all white.

Everyone else is tan and gray.

I'm also smaller than most Dwarf Hamsters.

Out of all my siblings I was the last one to get adopted.

My Mom told me I was silly to worry about it. She said being the last one was *not* because I looked different. She told me someone special would come along. That I would definitely be adopted soon and go to a good home.

She was right.

Mom was always right.

Now, I live in this big house with Lucy Alberts and her mom and dad, Frank and Mary Alberts.

And my new friends Pawsley the dog, and Catchoo the *cat!*

Catchoo was the first one to be taken in by Lucy. She was a stray, but is now happy here. She says she no longer feels the need to be anywhere else but here.

I still think about my hamster family. Sometimes I wonder if my 3 brothers and seven sisters have nice homes and new friends like I do.

And my Mom?

I still miss my Mom.

Since I was the last one to see her, I wonder if she also has a new home.

And if she is as happy as I am in mine?

"Pookie?"

"*AARGH!*"

Startled, I tumble off the first step – headfirst – landing on my back. All four feet straight up in the air.

"W-Wha...? You scared me Pawsley! What are you doing out here?"

"Geez! Sorry Pookie, but I was about to ask you the same question! You okay down there?"

Pawsley stares down at me from the top step.

As he tilts his furry head to one side, a frown creeps across his forehead.

"Why are you out here in the dark?" he asks. "It's the middle of the night!"

"I could ask you the same thing, Pawsley. Why are *you* out here in the dark? Why aren't *you* sleeping?"

"Thirsty. When I got up to get a drink, you weren't in your house. So, I came looking for you. Do you do this *every* night while everyone is sleeping?"

I have to wiggle around and struggle to get my feet back underneath me so I can stand up.

"I'm trying to figure out the best way to get downstairs," I answer. "I don't know if I should go down nose first, hanging on with my back feet? That would be the safest. But also, very slow … orrr …"

Staring at how far I have to go to get to the bottom, I continue with a teasing grin.

"… orrr … maybe … I should just have you *scare* me down each step!"

I glance back up at him to see if he catches my joke.

He's still frowning at me.

"Very funny."

He sighs and rolls his eyes at my attempt at humor.

"I know hamsters are awake at night, but that still doesn't explain *why* you're out here, and trying to get downstairs."

CHAPTER TWO

Nighttime is quiet and dark in our house.

Just like I like it.

Being a hamster means I'm nocturnal.

That means I *prefer* to be awake at night and sleep most of the day.

However, I do get up for snacks and maybe a drink of water.

I learned how to escape from my cozy house a while ago. I was curious about what was out there in the rest of our big house, and I figured out a way to explore!

Nighttime is perfect because everyone else is sleeping.

Everyone but me.

Except for tonight.

Pawsley!

I got caught!

Pawsley is still staring at me from the top step.

He's waiting patiently for my answer on *why* I'm out here in the dark, so I slowly say, "I want to check out the downstairs. It's only twelve steps to get down there. And then I can go anywhere I want!"

"That's true," Pawsley says, also speaking slowly. "But I hope you realize, that twelve steps *down*, means you also have to climb those same twelve steps back *up!* And then, to get back in your house on Lucy's desk, you have to climb up the lamp cord. *And* the lamp arm!"

He sits down as he's talking to me. When he sits, only his front paws are visible because of how furry he is.

And his paws are huge.

His big feet are the reason Lucy named him *Pawsley*.

He sighs as he continues. "That's a lot of climbing. Even for a strong hamster like you! And all before Lucy wakes up to go to school? You sure about this Pookie?"

He squints his eyes and his eyebrows move closer together into a worried frown.

"Yes, I'm sure," I answer impatiently.

Why am I explaining this to him in the middle of the night, I think to myself. *Why did he have to find me?*

Still frustrated, I continue. "Haven't started down yet because I haven't had a chance to practice stairs."

I look all around me, and swing both arms out wide as if to take in all the unknown possibilities.

"I've already checked out all the rooms upstairs, so it's time I expand my exploring. I even brought some extra snacks just in case it takes longer than I planned."

Lucy gives me sunflower seed treats each morning before she leaves for school. But instead of eating them right away, I've been saving them just for this occasion.

Pawsley sounds as worried as he looks when he asks, "Well, have you thought about what would happen if you can't make it back in time? You'd be stuck!"

"I *know*! And I did think about all of that. I should have started out sooner. And I should have found a way to practice the stairs. But I won't know if I can do this unless I try!"

As we're having this discussion, I notice a dark shadow creeping up behind Pawsley.

It's Catchoo, our cat-roommate.

She's all gray, and almost invisible in the dark.

Except for her glowing green eyes.

She silently slinks over to us to see what's going on.

"What's all the noise out here?" she hisses. "Some of us are trying to sleep, you know!"

Catchoo acts bothered and irritated. But we both understand she *has* to be included in whatever is going on.

Her curiosity makes her want to know everything that's happening, or what's about to happen.

Pawsley tells her why we're out here in the dark. "Pookie wants to go downstairs to *explore,* and I'm explaining to him what would happen if he doesn't make it back before Lucy wakes up."

"caaat-CHOO!" Catchoo sneezes, and backs away.

She's allergic to other animals. Like dogs.

But oddly not to hamsters.

Lucy named her *Catchoo* because it's what her sneeze sounds like.

"Bless you!" Pawsley and I both bless her at the same time.

She brushes a paw across her face from her ears down to the tip of her nose.

Then she says, "I don't know what the big deal is about going downstairs. You're down there every Saturday with all of us when Lucy cleans your house." She turns to Pawsley and impatiently continues, "Why don't you just give him a ride? If he's so insistent about being down there, get it over with."

To her, taking action is better than talking about an issue. "I'm going back to bed. And try to keep it quiet out here, would you?"

Without waiting for a response from either of us, she turns and disappears.

We watch as Catchoo quietly and gracefully heads back to bed. Her soft padded paws allow her to move around in silence.

We look at each other and both of us sigh at the same time.

Pawsley shrugs and says, "She's right, ya know. What do you think is down there that you haven't already seen?"

"I know you don't understand. You two can go anywhere you want, and anytime you want. But, when I'm down there, I'm always in my ball. It's frustrating!

I can't touch anything.

I can't run under the furniture.

I can't look behind any doors or check out any corners.

And I can't climb up on the couch to look out the window like you guys do!"

I'm on a roll now and my feelings come tumbling out. "You two don't know how lucky you are. You can run upstairs, or downstairs. And even go outside to play when Lucy's home. When you're in the backyard with her, I can hear you barking and having all kinds of fun!"

Pawsley stands up again, but doesn't say anything.

"I want some of that same freedom," I tell him. "I want to do what you guys get to do."

CHAPTER THREE

Being jealous of my friends is selfish ...and I know it isn't right.

But I can't help it.

"When I'm rolling around inside my ball, all I can do is stay on the floor. That's it! And everything that I think would be fun to check out or interesting to see, is all high up above me. It's not fair!"

Pawsley listens sympathetically. Then lays down with his head resting on his paws so he's closer to me. He looks like a big scruffy black and white stuffed toy.

"Okay, okay. I get it!" he says with a sigh. "But you know it's for your own good, don't you? You're so little, your ball keeps you from getting hurt. It's your protection."

I know he's trying to understand and I appreciate him listening to me.

Pawsley continues, "Hey, don't forget that you got to be in the hamster race at the pet store! And you won! *We* have never done anything like that! Neither one of us is an athlete like you are!"

His ears perk up as he raises his head. He gets excited talking about the race. He was there with Lucy and her parents. And he cheered for me like he said he would.

"You're famous, my little friend! You have a blue ribbon. And a trophy! Your picture is still hanging in the store! You beat other hamsters that were lots bigger and stronger than you. Catchoo and I haven't done *anything* like that! And *we* don't have any trophies. You're a star, and you should be very proud!"

He's right.

And I am proud.

I see my trophy and ribbon sitting right next to my house on Lucy's desk every day.

"Pookie, you've done things we could never do. Even you being here right now. Climbing out of your cage and getting down to the floor safely! That's pretty amazing, don't you think?"

He's right again.

"And you have prizes that *we'll* never have. But all in all, I think the three of us are pretty lucky to be adopted by Lucy. And for us to be together and to be friends is pretty great. You have no reason to be jealous."

Pawsley calms me down.

And I do have to agree.

"You're right Pawsley," I say slowly. "I shouldn't feel bad that you get to go outside to play. Lucy does put me on her bed to run around when she comes home from school. And she certainly can't pick you or Catchoo up and give you kisses on the top of your head the ways she does with me!" I say this with a grin. "I really am a lucky hamster. We're *all* lucky!"

I feel better now.

And I *am* grateful for my friends.

As a reminder of why I'm out here in the dark, I say, "But I still need to explore!"

"Well, I'm going down to the kitchen to get a drink," Pawsley says. "So, hop aboard if you want a ride down. I can save you a lot of time and energy."

Not too long after I was adopted, Pawsley gave me a lift up to my house. It's on Lucy's desk where she does her homework. Catchoo saw me climb up on top of my wheel when it was stuck and wouldn't turn.

She swatted at me and knocked me all the way down to the floor.

She made me think she was going to eat me!

Then laughed about it.

Pawsley's black and white fur looks scruffy and rough. But I learned that day, it's really very soft. He graciously lowered his head close to the floor so I could climb on. Then he stood up, and lifted me back up to the desk. I was able to climb up the lamp, and jump into my house.

Tonight, I wanted to go downstairs all on my own, but I've wasted too much time trying to make up my mind how to get there. And then all this talking with the two of them wasted even more time. I decide to take Pawsley up on his offer.

"Okay. I'll take that ride. Thanks, Pawsley."

He has to go down a few steps and turn around so his head is level with the step where I landed.

I jump onto the top of his head and grab his fur with all four paws. I hang on with all my might!

He's not the biggest dog I've ever seen, but he's a giant compared to me.

The ride down is like being on a bucking bronco at a rodeo! And he's not very quiet as he clunks down the stairs on feet that seem far too big for the rest of his body!

He tries to go slower than his normal pace, but it's still brain-jarring and bumpy. But at least it's quick!

We get to the bottom of the stairs, and he lowers his head to the floor for me to jump off. He goes to the kitchen to get a drink from his water bowl while I look around trying to decide where to go first.

So much to explore!

"Good luck Pookie," he says licking the last of the water droplets from his lips.

He turns to leave and says, "You're on your own now, my friend. See you in the morning."

He stops for a moment, and looks back at me saying, "Hopefully back in your house!"

It sounds like a warning.

I watch him bound up the stairs on furry feet that make him look like he's wearing big fluffy slippers.

So easy.

For him.

And so quick.

And now I'm alone once again.

CHAPTER FOUR

It's quiet in the living room.

And dark.

Only the glow of a distant streetlight coming in the window helps me get my bearings.

I hesitate for a moment.

Then set out to explore.

23

The fluffiness of the carpet is the same as it is upstairs. It feels good on my feet, and easy to walk on.

When I did all my exploring upstairs, I wasn't worried about being too far away from my house. I checked out *all* the rooms up there on a few different excursions and was able to get back into my house in plenty of time before morning.

Lucy's room is big enough that the three of us easily have enough space to share it with her.

It's nice that we can all be together.

Her mom and dad's room is big also. Big enough to have a treadmill for them to exercise on.

"I bet I can go faster on my wheel than they can on that machine," I say to myself.

I've seen them when they're on that machine. They never look like they're having fun.

Strange.

I *love* running on my wheel!

I love the speed and how fast I can go. I always pretend I'm running free in a field of sunflowers.

It makes me think of the sunflowers at the end of the race I won at the pet store. Even though they weren't real, it was still exactly like my dream.

I wonder, do they have people races like they have hamster races?

I'm excited to be down here finally.

All kinds of places to check out.

But I *am* a little concerned about getting back upstairs and into my house before Lucy wakes up in the morning.

And Pawsley warned me.

There's so much to see and I still have to figure out how to manage those stairs.

I have a plan … I'll scope out the living room tonight. And save the other rooms for future adventures.

Conquering those stairs will *also* be an adventure!

I have to make sure to leave enough time to climb back up.

And then I have to get back in my house before Lucy wakes up to go to school.

I don't want to get caught, and I certainly don't want Lucy to know I can get out of my house!

Thinking about that worries me.

But only a little.

CHAPTER FIVE

Pawsley likes to stand up with his big paws on the front window sill in the living room. I've always wondered what he sees out there that is so interesting.

When I'm on the floor in my ball there's no way for me to know what he sees or what he's looking at.

But tonight, I'm going to find out!

I'm going to look out that window too!

I'll figure a way to climb up on the couch. Then up onto the arm.

Then it's a short leap to the window sill.

I have a plan.

But the couch is leather.

And it's slippery.

Nothing to grab on to.

"Maybe...if I use the footstool first? Yes! that'll work. Wait ... why am I talking out loud to myself?"

I shake my head, and get to work.

The footstool is cloth. Lots of loops and fibers to grip. It's an easy climb up the side and on to the top.

Now a *big* jump over to the couch!

Deep breath ...

Focus ...

JUMP!

... and fall to the floor right in front of the couch.

PLOP!

Thank goodness for the soft carpet.

Not hurt ... just a little dazed.

"Okay. Let's try this again." I shake my head. ... *more talking to myself?*

I climb up the side of the footstool again. Up onto the top.

"I can do this. I know I can!"

This time I visualize myself over there on the couch.

Sitting on that cushion.

I take another deep breath.

And *jump*!

For a split second, I'm flying through the air!

I land on the edge of the cushion.

I try to grab something, anything, with my back feet.

But all I get is ...

AIR!

My front paws are straining to hold onto the slippery leather seat.

Finally, I swing a back leg up. I'm able to get a toe-grip on the cushion seam. Almost there ... almost there!

Finally.

I'm up!

WHEW! That was close!

Now up the arm of the couch, and then a leap to the window.

The throw pillow resting against the arm gives me perfect traction to climb up.

I can see the window sill.

So close.

But there's a gap between the couch and the sill.

"Piece 'a cake!" I say to myself.

Compared to how far I just jumped to the couch, this will be easy.

But, if I don't make it, it's a long way to the floor!

Another deep breath.

Focus.

JUMP!

Made it!

On the window sill, I walk back and forth trying to see outside.

It's dark out there.

Like it is in here.

Pawsley's nose prints are on the glass. He always stands up in the same spot to watch whatever it is he sees out there.

Moving closer, I stand up and lean on the glass for a better view.

I put my own nose print right next to his.

Mine is a cute little round circle.

His is a smeary oval from him looking side-to-side with his nose still on the glass.

I wonder if he'll notice.

I wonder if he'll think it's as funny to see them side by side as I do.

The leaves on the oak tree in the front yard create an eerie silhouette. They sway gently and silently in the night breeze.

A family of squirrels lives in that tree. They're the ones Catchoo was running from the night she got caught in the sprinklers.

Lucy found her the following morning on the front porch trying to dry off in the sun. She brought her inside and she's been here ever since.

I chuckle to myself thinking about Pawsley telling me that story on my first day here.

"What a sight that must have been!" Again, talking out loud to myself?

There's nothing much to see out the window.

No people out walking their dogs.

No cars driving down the street.

No kids playing.

It's quiet ... very quiet.

And dark.

Guess I'm the only one awake.

But at least now I know what it's like to look out the front window.

Pawsley will be impressed.

And both of our nose prints are right there, side by side.

Chapter Six

It's time to think about how to get back up the stairs.

I accomplished something huge by climbing up on the couch and jumping over to the window.

Can't wait to tell Pawsley and Catchoo. Now I'm tired.

I jump off the window sill back onto the couch.

So much easier getting down than it is getting up there!

Before I make the leap to the footstool, I notice something white stuck at the back of the couch cushion.

Popcorn? Must have been movie night last night for the Alberts! Yum! Lucy won't ever know she left me a treat!

Can't help but stay and enjoy this unplanned snack.

I think about Pawsley and Catchoo sitting right here with Lucy.

Watching TV.

While I was sleeping.

I wash my face and hands when I finish eating. Just like Mom taught me. I know I have to head back home.

Not only did I accomplish looking out the window, but I got a tasty treat for my efforts.

I slide down the edge of the couch, landing on the soft carpet. No need to jump to the footstool. Getting down is easy!

Now I'm nervous.

I head toward the stairs.

Can't waste any more time if I want to get home before Lucy wakes up.

Twelve steps … a long way up.

Only one way to complete a task.

Just *begin!*

I grip the carpet on the vertical face of the first step with my front paws, and pull myself upward.

Pushing with my hind legs, I grab the edge with one back paw.

And I'm up on top!

Just like I did on the footstool.

"That wasn't so hard," I say to myself.

Then up the second step and onto the top in exactly the same way.

Well, this is really easy! What was I so nervous about?

I take a little breather, and scamper across the width of the step to look through the banister, down to the floor below.

Then I glance up.

Still a long way to go!

Only ten more steps to the top.

Taking a deep breath, I continue to climb.

With each step I accomplish, it becomes a little more difficult.

I'm getting really tired.

By the time I get to step number nine, I'm exhausted!

Rest – I have to rest.

Only three more steps to go.

I look over the edge again to the floor, wayyyyy down below.

That's too scary looking down there!

I scurry back to the other side of the step where I feel safe and sit in the corner by the wall to rest.

I'll just close my eyes for a few seconds and catch my breath …

SO tired …

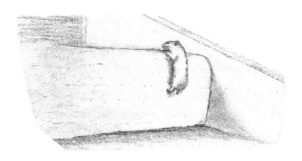

CHAPTER SEVEN

Huh?

Startled, I wake up to the sound of distant running water.

Where am I?

OH NO!

The sun isn't quite up yet but it's morning.

I recognize the sound of Lucy's dad taking a shower before he goes to work.

My heart starts to pound as I realize where I am and what I have to do in a *very* short amount of time.

I have only a few minutes before it's time for Lucy to wake up for school.

I can't get caught!

I just can't!

Still groggy, I stretch my legs, take a deep breath and start climbing again.

The last three steps I make in record time.

"I can't wait to tell Pawsley and Catchoo what I've accomplished! They'll be so proud of me," I say to myself as I get to the top.

Oh wait. I hope they're not awake yet. If they are, I'm in trouble ...

I run across the carpeted hallway to our bedroom.

Slowly ... I walk in ... hugging the edge of the half-open door.

I peek around the corner.

Lucy is still sleeping.

"Whew!" I breathe a sigh of relief.

But Pawsley's awake!

His ears perk up as he stares at me without raising his head.

And Catchoo's eyes are following me.

She's suspicious as I make a dash across the floor to the lamp cord hanging under Lucy's desk.

More climbing!

I grab the cord and begin my ascent, paw-over-paw.

Almost there.

I reach the top of the desk.

Lucy is beginning to wake up.

She turns over in bed, facing me.

But her eyes are still closed

Have to hurry!

Can't let her catch me!

Grabbing the lamp arm, I scramble to climb to the top where it hangs over my house.

"Made it!" I say to myself.

I jump, landing with a *fwoomp* into my soft bedding right in front of my wheel.

Last night I had jammed a bunch of fluff under it to keep it from turning.

It's how I'm able to climb up and out.

"G'morning Pookie!"

Lucy's awake, but still sleepy.

Yawning, she says, "You sure are awake early this morning."

Wide-eyed and holding my breath I stare at her.

Did she see me jump?

Hope not ...

"Looks like you've been a busy little boy last night. Why is all your fluff in a pile like that? Your wheel can't turn. Looks like it's stuck. Is that why you're awake?"

Lucy climbs out of bed, stretches, and says, "Here, I'll fix it for you."

She reaches in and smooths out my bedding as I watch her and realize what a close call I had.

She picks me up, gives me a hug and kisses the top of my head.

Why did I have to fall asleep on the stairs? This could have been a disaster!

I scold myself.

Catchoo and Pawsley are both frowning at me. They get up, stretch and yawn. I know I have to be prepared for them to scold me too.

The rest of the morning is like every other morning.

Soon Lucy's out the door to school.

Her mom and dad both off to work.

I hear Pawsley's big feet on the stairs coming back up to our room. I know Catchoo is right at his heels.

When they come in, I'm standing up ready to defend myself.

"Hi guys!" I try to sound cheery.

"Before you yell at me, let me point out that I *did* make it back in time! I know I cut it just a little close, but I made it. And yes, I do remember that you warned me, Pawsley."

I hang my head a little in a show of humility. Hoping – and waiting for them to say, *"Aw, that's ok. You're fine."*

But, no – they don't buy my act.

I get the evil eye from both of them! Then Pawsley lets me have it first.

"Do you realize you almost got caught? What were you thinking? I couldn't believe it when I woke up and you weren't back yet! I didn't want to move or go looking for you for fear of waking Lucy up. And having her see you were gone ...? I can't believe you ...!"

"B-b-but ..."

As I try to explain, Catchoo cuts me off, "Was this some sort of test Pookie? Were you trying to see how close you could come to getting caught? If so, that's so irresponsible! Lucy would have freaked out! And then what? I for one am so disappointed in you."

I roll my eyes and sigh. "But guys! If you'll just listen to me. I'm fine. Lucy's fine. And I'm home safe."

I start to talk faster in an attempt to impress them with my accomplishments, "You should have seen me climb those stairs! You would have been *so* proud. I know I didn't do it as fast as you two could, but I *did* it!"

But they're not impressed.

"*And* I got to look out the front window. What do you think about that Pawsley? Huh?"

I wait. Expecting some kind of interest.

Maybe some questions of *really?* or *how'd you do that?*

But, no.

They both just stare at me.

"And by the way, Pawsley," I continue in desperation. "I put my nose print on the front window right next to yours!"

Still no comment from either one.

"It's pretty cool. Yours is a big smear. And mine is right next to it. A neat little round one!"

I hold up a paw and bend my toes into a tiny circle to show him. "Oh yeah. And one paw print too. Right next to my nose print."

I raise my other paw like a high-five.

I continue trying to impress them.

To make them understand.

It isn't working.

"I started back up the stairs in plenty of time. But I guess all my climbing to get

43

up to the window, then down again, then climbing the stairs ... really made me tired. I made it up nine stairs. But then I had to stop to rest. Guess I was more tired than I realized."

Embarrassed, I hang my head and say sheepishly, "I accidentally fell asleep."

They continue to stare at me, not sure what to say.

"And do you know how scared I was when I looked over the edge? Down to the floor? And I saw how far I'd come? It *really* was scary! But exciting! I couldn't wait to tell you guys all about it!"

They're still frowning at me.

Both of them.

"Please don't be mad at me. It was hard work!" Pleading, I continue. "Look. I promise. It'll never happen again. I know it was a close call, but now I know what it takes to get up the stairs. So, I'll make sure I give myself more time *next* time."

I state my case, and look at them waiting for a sign they understand.

A sign they're not mad at me.

A sign they forgive me.

"Are we okay? Friends? My two very, *very* best friends? Are we buddies? Huh?"

Silence.

Still staring at me.

I wait with my toes crossed.

Finally, they look at each other and sigh.

Catchoo finally says, "Fine! But you said you thought your return was *a little* too close? Seriously?"

She shakes her head in disbelief. "If you EVER play it that close again, I will close the bedroom door so you can't get back in! *When* you finally make it back up here!"

Her back is arched, and her tail is standing straight up in the air. "You'd really be in a fix then, wouldn't you? Lucy and her parents would definitely find out! That would teach you a lesson! And don't think I won't do it!"

Pawsley gives her a quick surprised look. But he says nothing to contradict the harsh threat.

I secretly breathe a sigh of relief "Okay, okay. I get it! As I said, it won't happen again. Promise."

I give them a tired look and say, "Now, if you guys don't mind, I need to get some sleep. I'm exhausted!"

They both shake their heads and leave the room.

My eyes are starting to droop.

I get a drink, eat a little breakfast and snuggle into my bed. I can't help but smile to myself as I drift off to sleep.

I had a great adventure.

I made it back to my house – even tho I was a *little* late.

I made peace with my friends.

The only thing that would have been more exciting would be to find some sunflower seeds instead of the popcorn.

But the popcorn was a nice surprise.

CHAPTER EIGHT

I don't understand how Pawsley and Catchoo know how to tell time. But they do.

They run downstairs to wait by the front door when they know Lucy will be home from school and her parents, home from work.

When Lucy comes in, I hear all the meowing and happy barking. They miss her and want attention.

It's the same routine every day.

After they get hugs, and their ears ruffled, they all race upstairs into our room.

Catchoo brags to me about how much Lucy misses *her*.

I just shake my head and sigh.

Lucy says, "Hi Pookie! Did you miss me too!" She always greets me when she comes in. I sleep most of the day, so this is always a nice way to wake up.

I love her!

And I know she loves me back.

She puts her books on her desk next to my house. Then changes out of her school clothes.

"C'mon Pawsley, let's go outside. Only a short walk today tho. It's gonna rain. When we get back, we'll all go downstairs and play. You too Pookie! I'll put you in your ball so you can run around with us."

She giggles as she leaves with Pawsley wagging his tail, and smiling.

I know he doesn't care if he gets wet walking in the rain.

So why is it that he tries to hide under the bed when it's time for him to get a bath?

What's the deal?

When they come back, she puts me in my ball like she said she would. She carries me with both hands leading the way downstairs. She gently sets me on the floor in the living room.

In my ball. I sigh. ... *again* ...

Can't touch anything or climb up on anything.

But, it's okay.

At least I'm here with everyone.

Playing.

I use this time to roll around checking out other places. And to form a plan on where I'll go the next time I go exploring.

The dining room? Maybe ...

I could run under the table and chairs. Maybe find some crumbs to munch on. I can't do that now, because my ball won't fit.

The laundry room? Nah.

Been there before, and it's pretty boring. It's where Lucy washes my house on Saturdays.

Maybe the kitchen? Yes!

Lots of things to check out in there. And it's a tile floor instead of carpet!

"I think I'll go in there now while the others are occupied. Just to check things out." I say to myself.

Lucy giggles as she gives Pawsley a belly rub. He's on his back with all four legs spread out like he's flying.

He's ticklish and when she rubs his belly one leg looks like it's riding a bicycle.

Really fast!

He growls.

And groans.

And whines.

He makes some weird noises when he's having fun.

All while he's wiggling around on his back.

Catchoo watches as if she's bored.

As usual.

She glances over at me in my ball.

Acting like a predator, she begins to stalk me.

Closer and closer.

And then she *pounces!*

She has me captured between her front paws.

Staring at me – grinning.

"Would you just stop it Catchoo? Sometimes you can be very annoying!"

I know she's playing, but I can't move.

She laughs.

"It's not funny! How would you like it if I did this to you?"

As if I was big enough to bother her.

She really laughs at the thought of me being able to *pounce* on her.

She finally lets me go, and runs to Lucy to steal attention away from Pawsley.

Both she *and* Pawsley are now on their backs with legs stretched out in all directions.

Pawsley is still making his weird noises as Lucy plays with his paws.

And Catchoo meows with content as she gets a belly rub.

Now I can continue on into the kitchen where Lucy's mom is making cookies.

There're always good smelling things happening in here when her mom is baking.

I don't know what those smells are, but it makes my nose twitch.

Rolling around on the tile floor is easy.

And fast.

It's like the long hallway to the back door.

My favorite place.

If I get a good running start, I know I could fly right out the door into the backyard.

If only someone would leave the door open ...

Of course, that never happens.

But I still love the feeling of speed.

It's exhilarating when I go so fast, my feet can't hardly keep up!

I follow Lucy's mom's feet as she moves around the kitchen.

From the sink where she washes her hands.

To the oven where the cookies are baking.

To the counter top where the cookies are cooling.

As she turns quickly to grab a potholder, she accidentally kicks my ball!

I go spinning out of control as the room twirls around me!

"Lucy!" She has to yell to be heard over all the noise and giggling coming from the living room.

"Lucy! Come get Pookie! He's in my way here in the kitchen, and I don't want him to get hurt! I almost stepped on him!"

Lucy stops playing and runs to the kitchen to save me.

"How did you get out of my sight, Pookie? Good thing you're in your ball. You need to stay here where I can see you."

She puts me down next to Pawsley and Catchoo. They both stare at me like it was *my* fault their play was interrupted.

"Mom? Those cookies sure smell good! Can I have one? I want to go upstairs and finish reading my book."

From my ball back into my house.

We're all relaxing as Lucy sits on her bed with her knees propped up. Reading her book and enjoying her cookie.

She was right when she told Pawsley it was going to rain.

It's pouring!

Listening to the patter of raindrops hitting the window is a peaceful sound to me.

Thunder and lightning outside make our room inside feel snuggly.

It's cozy for all of us to be together.

I feel safe.

And watching my friends, I think they feel the same.

I close my eyes and snooze.

Chapter Nine

"You sure have been quiet the last few days Pookie? Everything okay?"

Pawsley is eyeing me suspiciously, like he can read my mind.

Lucy and her parents are gone for the day. School and work. So, it's just the three of us, relaxing in our room like any other normal day.

Catchoo is taking her midday nap.

I still want to check out the kitchen. I've only been there in my ball. I'm convinced there's lots of exciting stuff to discover.

But I know better than to mention wanting to get out of my house again – at least for a little while longer.

I'm back in the good graces of my friends, and I really don't want to press my luck.

Pawsley is still eyeing me suspiciously.

"I'm fine Pawsley. I was just thinking about how fortunate we are to have Lucy adopt all of us. Bet there's not too many other ten-year-old girls that would want to take care of the likes of the three of us! And isn't it amazing that we all get along? That we're friends?"

Pawsley nods in agreement. "She really does take good care of us. And you're right about all of us being friends. It's pretty amazing."

Catchoo gets up to move because her sunbeam keeps disappearing behind clouds. It's looks like it might rain again.

Usually she doesn't even have to wake up to move.

This time she gets up, stretches and stares at me as if she has something she wants to tell me.

"Why are you staring at me Catchoo?"

"I dunno. You're not acting normal. I think you're up to something."

She turns around. Plops down and spreads out again when the sun pops out from behind a cloud.

How does she do that? They both seem as if they can read my mind, I think to myself.

Pawsley is still looking at me.

He seems curious about why I didn't have a comeback to Catchoo's remark.

"Pookie? *Are* you up to something?"

"Why are you two so suspicious?"

"Because we know you. And can tell when you're not acting normal. And there has to be a reason."

He pauses to see if I deny it.

"I'm just sayin'. If you're going out again, remember my warning. And remember Catchoo's threat. *That* would not be good!"

I sigh out loud.

"Pookie, we just care about you. And want you to stay safe. Think about it! You're out there by yourself. In the dark. If you get hurt, who's going to help you?"

"Thank you Pawsley. I appreciate your concern. And Catchoo's also."

I see her open one eye as she pretends to be sleeping. I know she can hear me.

"But don't worry about me. I'll be fine. And I'll be careful. And when – or if – I go out again, I will be more responsible about getting back on time. I promise!"

Pawsley nods. And sighs.

"Alright. Just be careful, okay?"

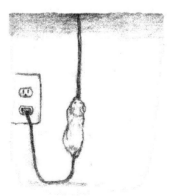

CHAPTER TEN

I'm restless.

Pawsley and Catchoo think I'm planning something and keep watching me suspiciously.

They're right ... I do have a plan.

Tonight's the night.

I can't stop thinking about exploring the kitchen. There's just so *much* in there to see!

It's midnight.

Everyone's sleeping.

The house is dark and quiet and I don't think I can wait any longer.

As quietly as I can, I climb up on the top of my wheel, hop up on the lamp, and slide down the arm to the desk. Then climb down the cord to the floor.

Nobody stirs.

I *run* across the room and out the door!

This is the fastest escape I'd ever done.

And the quietest.

Everything's good so far.

Now the stairs.

They're straight across from the bedroom door.

Without hesitating, I go right to the edge of the top step.

I jump down, landing on the cushy carpet of the second step.

Over to the edge.

It's an easy hop down to the third step in exactly the same way.

Before too long, I'm all the way to the bottom.

Without even thinking about being scared.

Easy-peasy!

Looking across the living room, I see the window I was able to climb up to and look out. Even from down here on the floor, I can see Pawsley's nose print.

And mine right beside it.

I feel proud.

Too bad I didn't think to point it out to him and Catchoo when we were all playing down here a few days ago.

He probably noticed it, but didn't want to say anything.

He'd have to admit to being impressed with my climbing skills.

It makes me smile remembering how difficult that climb was! But also, how much I accomplished.

Even tho I got in trouble with my friends, it all worked out okay.

And here I am again. I promised them I'd be careful, and I will be.

Wasting no time to go anywhere else, I scoot across the carpeted living room, and head straight to the kitchen.

Chapter Eleven

It's not as easy to walk on a smooth floor as it is on carpet like the living room.

Nothing to grip.

But the coolness of the tile feels good on my feet – better than the inside of my plastic ball.

I scout the perimeter of the kitchen and under the edge of the cabinets first. Hoping to find a few crumbs to munch on.

Maybe little bits of oatmeal flakes from the cookies Lucy's mom made.

Nothing.

I know she always makes sure the floor is clean. Especially with a furry dog and cat roaming free in the house.

"Tee hee!" I chuckle out loud.

She doesn't know there's a furry hamster roaming free also!

I make myself laugh sometimes.

But I don't shed, so there will be *no* trace that I've been here.

No one will ever know!

I continue to check out all the nooks and crannies under the edge of the cabinets anyway.

From somewhere close by comes a whiff of something that smells tempting.

And it's not the smell of baking cookies. Or the Alberts' dinner.

My night vision is pretty great. But it's my nose that leads me to a delicious aroma coming from a very small hole on the underside of the one of the cabinets.

I can't resist checking it out.

The hole is big enough for my head to fit through, so I cautiously poke my nose up inside.

"This is definitely where those yummy smells are coming from," I say out loud.

I continue to squeeze my head and front paws up through the hole to get a better view.

Not easy, but what a find!

I'm glad I make the effort.

The inside of the cabinet reminds me of the pet store where I came from.

Bags of Pawsley's food, Catchoo's food, and my food – all lined up neatly, side by side.

I'm a little smaller than a normal dwarf hamster, which now gives me an advantage. I *squeeeeze* the rest of the way up into the cabinet.

I'm ecstatic about my discovery, and can't wait to tell my friends!

Right next to Pawsley's food, is the bag of doggie cookies he goes so crazy over.

When Lucy offers him one, he does what she calls his *happy dance.*

All four feet prance in place, as if he can't contain the excitement of getting a treat.

Catchoo's bag of food smells like tuna. And the bag next to it has a picture of a cat smiling. I assume these are the cat treats she thinks are too disgusting to eat. She certainly does *not* smile when Lucy tries to get her to eat one.

She sticks her nose up, turns and walks away. There's an air about her that says, "*you must be joking!*"

Curious about why she doesn't like them, I chew a hole in the bottom of the bag – a hole big enough that a few treats tumble out.

"Hmmm ... not bad," I say to myself as I munch on one. "Soft ... chewy ... a little bit sweet ..."

I decide it's just Catchoo's cat-attitude, not the taste of the treat that makes her turn up her nose.

I chew a hole in the bag of her regular food, and *lots* of little nuggets come pouring out!

I jump back in surprise at the little mountain of cat food at my feet.

When I taste a piece, I realize I'm definitely not a tuna fan.

I climb up and over the pile to check out Pawsley's food. I chew a hole in his bag also.

But his food is bigger.

Nothing tumbles out.

I have to stick my head inside the bag, and *pull* the nuggets out.

His food is tasty.

I don't know what it's made of, but I'd eat it if I didn't have any of my own.

But I still like mine much better.

The bag of doggie treats Pawsley goes so crazy over has a picture of a black and white dog on it.

But his fur is smooth.

And shiny.

And he's smiling.

Pawsley is also black and white. And he smiles a lot too.

But Pawsley's scruffy fur is certainly not smooth! Or shiny!

Pawsley always looks like he got caught in a windstorm. His hair sticks out all over. Even after his bath. That's his natural look, and it's never any different.

The bag of his treats is thicker than the other bags. It's hard work to finally chew a hole big enough for a few cookies to fall out.

The effort isn't worth it – his treats are nothing *I* would do a happy dance over!

I walk around the growing piles of different foods toward the back of the cabinet.

There in the far corner, is a bag of *my* favorite treats!

I can't believe I found a stash of sunflower seeds! It's the same kind of bag with the same picture of sunflowers that I remember from the pet store.

It was always right beside our house where I could see it when I was running on the wheel. I would always imagine I was running free in a field of sunflowers. And eating as many seeds as I wanted.

And now I've found the source of where Lucy gets the few she gives me in the morning before she leaves for school.

I eagerly chew a hole in the corner of the bag.

They come gushing out creating a pool of black and white striped seeds that cover my feet!

I can't believe I'm standing in my favorite dream!

My discovery makes my whole trip worth it. I decide to stuff my cheeks as full as I can.

"This is so exciting! When I get back home, I'll have a huge pile I can stash in a corner."

I'm ecstatic.

"Now I can't help but talk to myself out loud! Sounds funny with my mouth full."

No more waiting for Lucy to give me two or three each day. I can have as many as I want any time I want!

I know they're supposed to be *treats,* but I don't care!

I decide to leave with my treasure, and head back home.

I'll save the rest of my exploring for another time. There's plenty of other nights to explore more!

I make my way around the food piles to the small hole at the front of the cabinet.

"Uh-oh!"

I stuffed so many seeds in my cheeks, my head is now twice it's normal size!

I can't get back through the hole!

"Ppppssyyy? Ccthoooo?"

I try to call out to Pawsley or Catchoo for help. But my cheeks are so full, the only sound that comes out is a muffled mumble.

I was so quiet when I left, they probably don't even know I'm gone.

And they're too far away to hear me anyway. So even if I could yell, they'd never hear me.

The only thing I can think to do is to start shelling the seeds I stuffed. Without the shells, the seeds won't take up as much room in my cheeks.

I start spitting the shells out and slowly my head gets smaller.

But still not small enough.

I decide to swallow a few, but only enough to get through the hole.

I *love* sunflower seeds so much, it's impossible to eat just a few!

Before I know it, I've eaten *all* the ones I shelled!

I don't know how much time has passed, but I can't go home without bringing some back with me. I return to the pile and scoop up some more.

I'm feeling a little queasy, and decide to rest a little before going back. Once again, I peel some seeds, but not as many this time.

Carefully, I stuff them back into my cheeks, making sure my head doesn't get so big that I can't get back through the hole.

"There!" I say to myself.

I'm satisfied I've solved the problem.

I think I'll fit through the hole now. But I really don't feel too good. I'll just sit here and close my eyes – just for a minute ...

I snuggle up in the corner next to the hole and shut my eyes.

And wait for my belly ache to go away.

Chapter Twelve

"Wh ...? What's going on?"

Startled, I wake up to see daylight peeking in around the edge of the cabinet door. Pawsley is barking. Lucy is crying, and her mom is trying to calm her down.

I'm worried about Lucy, but I'm too scared to move.

And my belly still hurts from eating too many sunflower seeds.

I guess I fell asleep! How did this happen?

Realizing where I am, I panic!

"I'm in big trouble now!" I whisper to myself.

I look around and see the mess I made with sunflower shells all over. And the bags of Pawsley's and Catchoo's food and treats spilling out on the cabinet floor.

I stay quiet, holding my breath, not knowing exactly what to do.

"Pookie! Where are you?" Lucy is walking around, searching and calling my name in between sobs.

"Where could he be, Mom? How could he get out of his house?"

Lucy's mom is moving chairs, looking behind doors, and calling my name also.

She's trying to comfort Lucy by assuring her I'll be alright.

"He'll be fine, Lucy. You know he sleeps during the day. So, if he somehow did get out, he's just curled up in a corner somewhere, dreaming sweet little hamster dreams. He'll wake up thirsty and come out when he's ready."

Her mom tries to sound positive, and calm Lucy down.

"You have to go to school, and we have to go to work. I'll bet he'll be waiting for us when we all get home later today!"

"No, Mom! Please? I don't think I should go to school today! I need to stay home and search for him!"

She begs her mom to let her stay home.

Lucy's dad gives her a hug, and says, "Lucy, are you sure he's not in his cage? Remember when we got him? I told you since he's all white, he'd blend in with all his white bedding, and you wouldn't be able to see him. Maybe he's just hiding."

"No, Daddy. He's always awake when I leave, and he just wasn't there this morning."

"Well," her dad says gently. "Don't worry, we'll find him eventually. And like your mom said, if he's out somewhere, he'll sleep all day. Besides, I don't think he'd be able to get down the stairs! I'm sure he'll be in your room when you get home. So, you do need to go to school. And your mom and I need to go to work."

Lucy wipes the tears from her eyes, and sadly leaves for school without saying her usual goodbyes to Pawsley and Catchoo.

A few minutes after she leaves, I hear her parents leave for work.

I sit very still.

Inside the cabinet.

Waiting.

Still not knowing what to do.

It's quiet after the Alberts leave.

Until I hear Pawsley's sniffing.

Still I remain quiet.

His sniffing gets louder.

And closer.

I realize he's right outside the cabinet door!

Afraid to even breathe, I don't move!

"Catchoo?" Pawsley calls to her. "Come over here please. Do you smell anything odd?"

I can imagine her sauntering over, trying not to get too close to Pawsley when she yowls and wrinkles up her nose.

"Oh, yuck! It smells like those cat treats Lucy tries to get me to eat! They're terrible! Is that smell coming from this cabinet? Why would they start to smell all of a sudden? Maybe Lucy left the bag open?"

I'm sure they're giving each other a knowing look as the same thought enters their heads ... at the same time.

Together, they yell, *"POOKIE!"*

Catchoo grabs the edge of the cabinet door with her paw, and yanks it open.

A mix of all of our food tumbles out onto the floor.

I'm standing on my hind feet, cheeks still stuffed with seeds, wide-eyed and grinning.

"Hi, guys! Were you looking for me?"

I try to sound casual as I continue.

"Would you like a couple of treats? I have whatever you want right here."

I make a sweeping motion with my arms at all the bags behind me. I kick a few extra nuggets to the floor.

They glare at me, ignoring the food.

And the treats.

Pawsley frowns as he scolds me. "Why are you here? Why aren't you in your house? You made Lucy cry! She searched everywhere for you. She's so worried, she wanted to miss a day of school. She *never* misses school! I warned you the last time, didn't I?"

"Yes. Yes, you did Pawsley. I'm *so* sorry, but I found the sunflower seeds and ate too many. And I also ate a little of all your food. I wanted to see what it tasted like."

I hang my head, trying hard to explain and wishing they would understand.

"I didn't mean to fall asleep, but I got a belly ache. I *still* have a belly ache."

My hope for sympathy from my two friends doesn't work.

They look at each other.

Then back at me.

Then shake their heads in disbelief.

Catchoo arches her back and glares at me. "I'm glad you have a belly ache!" She hisses. "Serves you right for making Lucy cry. She's really worried about you, Pookie! And look at the mess you made! How are you going to clean this up?"

I look back at the little mountains of food, and realize how much trouble I'm in. I could sure use their help.

Instead, they both turn around and leave. Dog food, cat food, and sunflower seeds are scattered all over the cabinet floor because of the holes I chewed in the bags.

What was I thinking?

I was so excited last night ...

I guess I *wasn't* thinking!

There's nothing I can do about cleaning up inside the cabinet.

At least Catchoo opened the door so I didn't have to worry about squeezing back through that tiny hole again.

I stuff a few more shelled seeds in my cheeks and jump out.

Trying to ignore all the food I kicked out onto the floor, I head back to the stairs.

Pawsley and Catchoo have abandoned me and are most likely back up in our room.

I look up at the stairs ...

and begin my climb.

CHAPTER THIRTEEN

The stairs seem a lot harder to climb looking up from the bottom, than they do looking down from the top.

But I have no choice, and grab the carpet on the first step.

I pull myself up with all my might.

Paw-over-paw I make it to the next step.

My belly still aches.

But it feels better when I can stop to catch my breath.

Looking up to the top, I realize I can't rest too long, or this journey will take all day!

My cheeks are heavy with all the extra seeds I stuffed. But I'm determined.

I take a deep breath, and continue climbing.

It takes all my strength to pull myself up each step. Even though I'm in trouble, I can't help thinking that once again, no one sees what I'm doing.

And my climbing is pretty awesome!

But my friends are a long way from being impressed with me!

I'm exhausted when I finally reach the top.

As I turn around to look back at what I've accomplished, I feel proud of myself. But then I remember that I made Lucy cry and both of my friends are mad at me.

And there's a mess on the kitchen floor.

And inside the pet food cabinet!

I have to fix the problems I caused.

But all I want to do right now is get back in my house and sleep.

Catchoo and Pawsley are lounging on the floor, soaking up the sunbeams streaming in the window of our room. They're blocking my path to Lucy's desk where I have to climb the lamp cord to get to my house.

As I get closer, they both raise their heads and stare at me, waiting for me to talk first.

"Hi Pawsley. Hi Catchoo. Guess what! I climbed the stairs again. In record time! You should have seen me!"

I was right.

They're not impressed.

And they don't answer.

"Are you still mad at me? I'm sorry I caused so much trouble. And I'm sorry I made Lucy cry. I didn't mean to fall asleep in the cabinet. But I ate too much of all the different food, and got a belly ache. Did I mention I found the bag of sunflower seeds? You remember how much I love them, don't you? So, I stuffed my cheeks full. *Then* my head was too big to get back thru the hole. *Then* I had to eat some of the seeds to make my head get smaller. And *then*, I got more of a belly ache. It hurts a lot. Have you guys ever had a belly ache? Huh?"

I'm trying hard to explain.

I'm talking too fast.

It all comes out sounding like excuses.

They both just stare at me.

Finally, Catchoo stands up and says, "We don't care too much about how you feel right now, Pookie. Pawsley warned you the last time about getting back here before Lucy wakes up. And did you forget that you *promised?* You blew it! And how do you plan to fix that mess you made?"

"I don't know. Right now, I just need a nap. I want to get back in my house, and go to sleep."

All I can think about is my nice soft bed. I want to rest and get rid of this belly ache.

"I didn't mean to make Lucy cry. And I didn't mean to make a mess. And I didn't mean to upset you both."

I have no idea how to make it up to them, but right now, I need sleep.

They're both standing now, allowing me to make my way to the desk.

Neither of them offers to help.

They watch as I climb, paw-over-paw once again. Up the lamp cord to the top of the desk, then shimmy up the lamp arm, and jump into my house. I land in my nice soft white fluff. Exhausted!

I don't even bother getting into my comfy bed. I just bury myself right where I land.

And fall fast asleep.

CHAPTER FOURTEEN

The next thing I'm aware of is Lucy sighing and plopping her books down on her desk.

Peeking through my fluffy bedding that covers me, I see her give Pawsley a pat on his head, and scratch Catchoo's ears. She's sad as she tells them I'm missing.

"Our little friend Pookie is gone, and I don't know where he is. He's always awake when I leave *and* when I get home. He's so cute when he stands up on his hind feet to get a sunflower treat. This morning, he just wasn't there. He must have got out somehow. Maybe you guys can help me look for him?"

They both watch as she puts her hand in my house to smooth out what she must think is just a pile of my white bedding. When I slowly raise my head, she jumps back and shouts in surprise.

"*POOKIE!* You're here! Where have you been? Were you hiding? How come I couldn't see you?"

Lucy's dad hears her shouting, and rushes in to see what's going on. "Lucy? What's the matter? Are you okay? Is everything alright?"

"Look, Daddy! Look! It's Pookie! He's right here in his house! He's not missing after all! I think he was just hiding!"

There are happy-tears in her eyes as she picks me up.

She brushes off the remains of white fluff sticking to my fur and hugs me repeatedly.

And gives me lots and lots of kisses on the top of my head.

"Oh, Pookie! I thought you were gone forever. I'm so happy you're still here. I'm sorry I didn't see you! Daddy was right, you're the same color as your white bedding. You blended so much I couldn't see you! I missed you!"

Lucy's dad sighs and smiles as he looks on.

Her mom comes running in to see what all the fuss is about. When she sees Lucy holding me, she smiles too. "Oh, thank goodness he's alright."

"I told you he'd be okay," her dad says. "And I'm glad you remembered that I said this might happen. That's why I thought *Spooky* would have been a good name for him when you adopted him. He's like a disappearing little ghost!"

Her dad laughs, and because Lucy is still holding me, when he hugs her, he hugs us both.

It makes me smile with relief.

Pawsley and Catchoo give each other a knowing look, and shake their heads in disbelief.

I'm happy that everything is fine now with Lucy. And for now, I'm safe.

She and her parents believe I was in my house, sleeping the entire time.

I'm still worried about the mess of food on the kitchen floor.

And in the cabinet.

But I have no way to fix it.

I feel terrible about causing Lucy so much worry, and I feel *really* terrible that my friends are still upset with me.

Lucy's happy again, and takes Pawsley out for a walk.

Catchoo and I are alone, and I try to apologize. She's not interested in talking to me, and goes back to lounging in the sunbeams.

"Catchoo. I'm sorry. I'm really, *really* sorry. But I don't know why you guys are still mad at me."

I plead with her.

"I made it back to my house on my own. Lucy's fine. She doesn't know that I was out. So, doesn't that make up for what happened?"

She doesn't even raise her head to answer me. "No, it doesn't Pook. Even though we don't understand why you want to get out and explore, we both helped you. Because we're friends. And friends help each other.

"All that climbing helped you get stronger, which also helped you win that hamster race a few months ago – if you remember. We don't care that you get out at night. But, it's *your* responsibility not to get caught. Or make Lucy and her parents worry. You *promised* us both the last time. Do you remember that? You broke your promise. You blew it!"

"But I said I'm sorry. I didn't do it on purpose. I'm back. I'm safe. Lucy's happy. And nobody had to search for me. It won't happen again, so could you please not be mad at me anymore? How much do I have to apologize before you believe how sorry I am?"

Pawsley is back from his walk, but he ignores me when I also try to apologize to him. "Pawsley, you know how much I appreciate all you and Catchoo have done for me. But, being friends is more important than anything. And I don't like it when you won't talk to me!"

He turns, looks me straight in the eye, and says, "I'm not mad, Pookie. But I'm sure disappointed that you can't keep a promise. That's the same as lying. How can we *ever* trust you again?"

He's right.

If someone made me a promise, and then didn't keep that promise, I would feel the same way.

"*And.* You should know Catchoo and I ate all the food you kicked out of the cabinet at us. So, we cleaned up the mess you made on the kitchen floor while you were sleeping."

I'm shocked.

And very grateful.

"Oh, you guys! How can I ever thank you for doing that! You two are the best!"

"But ..." Pawsley stares at me as he continues. "You should also know, that Lucy and her mom still found the *big* mess inside the cabinet!"

I hold my breath, waiting to hear what else he's going to say.

"They think it was me and Catchoo that did that! They think it was *us* that made that mess! We both got scolded. Then they moved all the food to a cabinet higher up. They no longer trust *us*. You not only ruined it for yourself, my little friend, but you got us in trouble!"

"Oh, no!! I'm so sorry! Catchoo, why didn't you tell me what you guys did? I feel terrible. I guess I owe you both! Big time! How can I make it up to you? I'll do anything you want. Just tell me!"

I *really* messed up. Not only can I no longer gather all the sunflower seeds I want when I get out again, but my friends got in trouble because of *me*.

How selfish! I never gave a thought to what effect my actions might have on my friends!

I'm so ashamed.

And embarrassed.

I have to do something to make it up to them. Somehow, I have to prove to them that I *can* be trusted.

I make a promise to myself that I will *never* let them down – ever again!

I decide I need to lay low and not even think about going out exploring at night.

At least for a little while...

CHAPTER FIFTEEN

It's been quiet the last few days. Everything seems to be back to normal.

My friends aren't mad at me anymore.

But they still don't trust me yet.

I'm anxious to get out of my house again. I want to go back downstairs and continue my exploring.

Now that I have experience navigating the stairs, I'm comfortable going down and back up again.

I'll make sure I get back home in plenty of time.

My goal is to get out like I did the last time. Neither Pawsley nor Catchoo will be aware that I'm gone.

Quick.

And quiet!

There's *no way* I want to cause more problems. Or get them – or me – in trouble.

I learned my lesson.

Losing their trust was the worst thing I've ever done.

I need to prove to them that I can be trusted once again.

I get busy with the process of getting out.

Stuffing my fluffy bedding under the wheel so it doesn't turn.

Climb up on top of it.

Grab the lamp.

Hoist myself out.

Slide down the lamp arm to the desk.

Shimmy down the cord to the floor.

I've done this enough times now that it seems ordinary.

And I'm very quick.

Scooting across the floor and stopping at the door, I take a look back before leaving.

I will not make any mistakes!

I will be back before they even know I'm gone!

Catchoo is curled in a ball in her bed on the floor.

Pawsley is stretched out across the foot of Lucy's bed.

Snoring.

Paws twitching as if he's chasing some squirrels.

He must have some exciting dreams when he sleeps.

The stairs are right across the hall from our bedroom.

No more wasting time.

I head straight for them.

Stopping at the top, I look back at our bedroom door one more time to make sure no one has discovered I'm out.

To make sure Pawsley didn't follow me like he did before.

And to make sure Catchoo isn't slinking about somewhere!

Alone in the dark, I hop down onto the first step.

Easy.

And so silent.

At the edge looking down, I make the jump to the second step.

Feels so good to be out again!

Just as I'm about to make the jump to the third step, I see an eerie glow coming from somewhere downstairs.

"Wait ... what is that?" I say to myself.

I stop. Dead still.

My ears straining to hear the least little sound.

Cautiously, I peer thru the banister at the edge of the steps.

Are Lucy's parents awake?

Walking around downstairs for some reason?

I hear nothing.

Silence.

Then the strange glow begins to move.

It scurries across the walls.

It hits the ceiling in the living room.

It hesitates at the bottom of the stairs.

It disappears toward the kitchen.

Then comes back again.

Someone or some*thing* is down there!

I'm scared.

My heart is pounding.

I don't know what to do.

Is my family in danger?

I have to warn them!

Something's not right!

Chapter Sixteen

The strange light continues to bounce all over. From one downstairs room to the next.

My heart is still racing as I scramble back up to the top of the stairs.

I'm yelling and screaming as loud as I can as I run back into our room.

"Pawsley! Pawsley! Help!"

I jump up and down, waving my arms frantically trying to get him to wake up.

He's sound asleep. And I can't scream loud enough for him to hear me!

Now I wish I hadn't been so successful *not* waking anyone when I got out tonight.

I have to find a way to warn them.

Running over to Catchoo's bed on the floor, I continue to yell and jump up and down.

"Catchoo! Catchoo! Wake up Catchoo!"

I jump up on her head.

She opens her eyes but doesn't move.

"Why are you on my head? And what are you screaming about? What is your problem now Pookie? I was asleep!"

She's clearly annoyed. I hop down in front of her face and continue excitedly.

"Catchoo! Wake up! There's something downstairs you have to see! Hurry! Come with me!"

"You're out again? What kind of mess did you make this time?"

"No, no, no! No, Catchoo, I think we're *all* in trouble! There's a weird light downstairs. Hurry! I'll show you!"

She doesn't believe me.

And still doesn't trust me.

But slowly, she gets up and follows me as I sprint to the head of the stairs.

"Look! Look down there What do you think it is?"

"How do you know that's not Lucy's mom or dad? They could've caught you being out you know."

"Catchoo! Listen to me. It's not them. There's no sound. It's quiet! Look! The light is moving all over the place. I'm telling you! Something's wrong!"

"Wha ...? How long ago did this start?"

"Only a few minutes ago. I was just going to go down and check out the rest of the kitchen. I only got down a couple of steps when I saw the light! I'm scared!"

Catchoo gives me a suspicious look and says, "You were going down to the kitchen? *Again?*"

She shakes her head, as she watches the light crawl around the walls, into the other rooms. When it tries to come up the stairs, she jumps back and whispers, "Whoa!"

"I tried to wake up Pawsley, but he can't hear me. And I can't reach him up on Lucy's bed. Catchoo, you have to go wake him up. NOW! He'll know what to do!"

She runs back to our room with me following her. I know she's scared now too. Her ears are flat against her head. And her tail is straight up in the air.

She jumps up on the bed where Pawsley is sound asleep. She yowls at him and paws at his nose.

"*caatCHOOO!*" she sneezes being so close to him.

"*caatCHOOO!*" she sneezes again but continues, "Pawsley! Wake up!"

She bites on his ear till he jumps in surprise. "What's going on?"

He looks at her, and then sees me on the floor jumping up and down on my hind legs.

"What are you two up to?"

"Shhh! Be quiet, but you have to wake up. And come with us! Pookie saw something downstairs! And so did I."

"What do you mean *saw something*? What kind of mess did you make now, Pookie?"

"I didn't do anything Pawsley. Please! Just come with us – NOW! Something's wrong!"

Catchoo prods him again and says, "SHHHHH!"

Suspicious, he steps quietly down from Lucy's bed and follows us to the top of the stairs.

The eerie light is still moving, darting in and out of the rooms downstairs.

He stares for a moment.

Then his body tenses.

He lowers his head, and his ears are back.

I have never seen him like this.

A slow quiet growl begins deep in his throat.

His lip starts to curl into a snarl.

We both watch wide-eyed as our gentle friend turns into a fierce aggressor.

"What do you think it is Pawsley?" I ask timidly.

He doesn't answer.

His hackles are up on the back of his neck.

The muscles in his shoulders flex as he slowly and steadily starts his decent down the stairs.

He's not afraid to confront whatever the threat is.

I'm certain he will protect this family no matter what.

His growl goes deeper.

And fiercer.

His eyes sharp and piercing.

His ears alert for any unfamiliar sound.

As he reaches the bottom step, he stops.

Frozen.

Tense.

Ready for an attack.

With his head low, a deep snarling bark starts in the back of his throat and becomes a thunderous rumble.

Still at the top of the stairs with Catchoo, I realize with this much commotion, Lucy and her parents will be awake in no time.

I don't want to get caught outside my cage. I scurry back into our dark bedroom and hide until I can safely get back home.

Just as I do, Lucy jumps out of bed frightened and breathing hard.

Her dad is up and frantically turning on lights.

Her mom runs to Lucy, gathering her in her arms to protect her.

Her dad says, "You two stay right here! I'll go see what's going on downstairs. Call 9-1-1!"

He runs down the stairs, grabbing a golf club from the hall closet.

Lucy's mom whispers, "Are you alright Honey? Do you know what Pawsley is barking at?"

"No, Mom. I was sleeping and all of a sudden I hear Pawsley barking. Like I've never heard him bark before! I thought I was dreaming. He sounds really mean! Mom, there's something really bad going on down there!"

"Don't be scared. I'm right here, and Daddy is checking things out. We'll all be fine. Come here Catchoo."

Catchoo joins the two of them on Lucy's bed. She curls up in Lucy's lap.

Lucy is so distracted and scared, she doesn't even notice I'm not in my house.

Then Catchoo sees me under the desk. She jumps off Lucy's lap and runs back to the top of the stairs.

"Catchoo! Wait!" Lucy's mom warns her in a loud whisper. "Don't go down there!"

They both follow her, giving me time to find a better hiding place.

The three of them sit at the top of the stairs. Waiting.

Lucy looks back into our room and says to her mom, "I hope Pookie's okay? I hope he's not scared too."

Catchoo saved me from being seen by dashing out of the room. I have to find a better hiding place until I can safely climb back in my house.

Without being discovered.

I hear Lucy's dad checking out all the rooms downstairs. The strange light is gone, but Pawsley is still barking. "Pawsley? What's the matter Boy? What do you see?" He's trying to calm him down.

Taking a chance, I make a mad dash out into the hall so that I won't miss what's going on downstairs. Nobody notices.

I hide in the corner by the banister, completely out of site in the shadows. But still with a full view of the downstairs.

Pawsley continues to snarl and bare his teeth while staring at the window.

Lucy's dad is still checking the other rooms. Trying to figure out what he's barking at. "Do you see something? Somebody out there? Good Boy!"

CHAPTER SEVENTEEN

The police arrive with lights flashing, and sirens blaring.

One officer is inside, talking with Lucy's dad. "No, Sir. I didn't see anyone. We were all sleeping when Pawsley woke us up by barking like crazy. Never heard him bark like that before. He sounded like he wanted to bite somebody's leg off."

The officer looks at him and smiles.

"Well, he's the best kind of watch dog to have. A trusted friendly pet. But willing to face danger head on when his family is threatened."

Pawsley glances up at him, still alert and suspicious.

The second officer comes in from checking all around outside.

"Mr. Alberts, I found muddy footprints on your front doorstep and also at your back door. Looks like someone was trying to find a way in. Good thing you're vigilant about keeping your doors locked at night."

Lucy's mom draws Lucy closer.

We're all still sitting at the top of the stairs.

They have no idea I'm here with them.

"And there are deep boot prints outside your front window. Also found a flashlight. Looks like whoever was out there, dropped it when he ran. Probably got scared off when your dog started barking. Shows he was most likely looking in your windows to see if it was a good house to break into. All this rain we've had made the ground soft enough that the guy left perfect footprints. Nice you've got such an alert watchdog."

Pawsley is quiet now. He glances up to see Lucy and her mom sitting on the top step. With Catchoo still on Lucy's lap.

He doesn't see me.

When Lucy's dad finishes telling the police the details of the night, they're ready to leave.

"Your family is safe Mr. Alberts. Knowing there's a dog here, it's unlikely the prowler would want to come back. We've had other reports of suspicious activity in the area. But now we have proof there really is someone out there. We'll have patrol cars making frequent rounds from now on until we catch him. We never had proof before, but now we have his boot prints. And his fingerprints on the flashlight and your front door. Don't worry. We will catch him."

As the officers head to the door, they each give Pawsley a pat on the head.

The one who found the flashlight takes an extra moment with him. He holds his head in both hands, looks right into his eyes and says, "Good job keeping your family safe! You're a good boy Pawsley. Keep up the good work!"

Pawsley gives him a soft "WOOF" and licks his hand to thank him.

The first officer says, "We know how disturbing all of this is. So, I hope it's not too late for you all to try to get back to sleep. And feel safe. Looks like you're in good shape here with a watchdog like Pawsley."

As he hands Mr. Alberts his card, he gets a call from another patrol car in the neighborhood.

"Well, it sounds like we may have caught him already thanks to you Mr. Alberts. And Pawsley here. They picked up a guy running down the street with muddy clothes and boots. He tried to convince the officer he was just out taking a walk. I think you can all rest easy now. You have my card, so don't hesitate to call us if you ever see anything suspicious or strange around your neighborhood."

After they leave, Lucy runs downstairs and throws her arms around Pawsley's neck.

"Pawsley! You're so brave!! You're such a good dog! How did you know there was someone out there?"

CHAPTER EIGHTEEN

Lucy's mom follows Lucy downstairs. With a sigh of relief, she says, "How about some hot chocolate for all of us? We'll just relax for a minute so we can all get back to sleep."

Catchoo and Pawsley watch them go to the kitchen, then come up the stairs, looking for me.

"Am I in trouble again?" I ask as they see me step out from behind the banister.

Catchoo looks startled when she sees me. "What are you doing? Why are you still out? You better get back in your house before Lucy comes up to go to bed!"

I follow them into our room, and quickly climb up and into my house.

"By the way, Catchoo, thanks for distracting Lucy and her mom so they didn't see me. I wasn't sure where to hide."

I'm sincere as I say to both of them, "I'm *really* sorry if I caused problems again. Please don't be mad at me for getting out tonight. I was so careful. And I knew how important it was to be able to get back in time. I didn't forget your warning, Catchoo. But mainly, I didn't want to disappoint either of you – again!"

Catchoo jumps up on the desk to be next to my house.

"Pookie, you're not in trouble. If it weren't for you warning us, that prowler probably would have broken in!"

"Oh ... well ... I didn't really do anything. You guys would have heard him eventually without me. And it would have turned out the same." I try to humbly dismiss her praise.

Pawsley is quiet, staring at me. He sighs and gets up on Lucy's bed. We're all at the same eye level now.

He looks directly at me, and in a serious tone says, "You're not in trouble. Catchoo is right. If it weren't for you, this night would have ended completely different. *You* are responsible for saving this whole family."

"But Pawsley ... I didn't do anything! I was really scared. I was screaming as loud as I could and couldn't wake you up! It was Catchoo that woke you. And then you were so brave going down there. I never heard you bark like that before."

"Do you hear what you're saying Pookie? It was *you* who discovered the light. And yes, it was you who woke up Catchoo so that she could wake me up! But *you're* the hero!"

We sit quietly staring at each other, letting what happened tonight sink in.

Pawsley continues. "Remember when I told you that I was concerned about you being out by yourself? I asked if you had thought about what would happen if you got hurt. How would you get help? Or if you had some sort of problem, who could you call? If I can't hear you when you're right here in the same room, how would I hear you from way down there? Don't you think tonight qualifies as a *what if* moment? So, *what if* you had already made it downstairs? And *what if* that prowler had made it inside. You would not have been able to make it back up all the stairs in time to warn Catchoo. Or me."

He pauses, looking at me with a worried look on his face. Catchoo lays down next to my house, not saying a word.

"I don't even want to think about all the things that could have gone wrong. I can't tell you what to do, but please take this seriously and think about what you're doing. I will defend this family against *any* danger, *any* time! You and Catchoo are my family along with Lucy and her parents. But there's no way for me to know where you are or what you're doing when I'm sleeping. I can't know what goes on in the dark. Downstairs. Or even up here when you're so quiet about escaping."

"You're right Pawsley. I agree, and I'm so sorry. It was a good thing I didn't make it all the way down there. That would have been a disaster. Guess I was lucky." I sigh and hang my head in dismay.

"I'm so grateful to be in this family. I'll stay in my house and be safe from now on. No more exploring!"

"Well," Pawsley continues, "I have to admit that this time, it was a good thing you were out, Pookie."

Catchoo agrees. "If it weren't for you being out, this night may have ended differently. So, I think Pawsley's right. Maybe you should just let us know what your plans are ahead of time. Then we won't worry ... not that *I* worry."

She hops down off the desk onto the bed. "And then you won't have to be jumping on my head anymore either!"

I look at her and can't help but smile. She tries hard not to let on that she cares about me. But it's obvious she does.

"I guess that means we're a team?"

They both look at me, then at each other. We all nod in agreement.

Catchoo stares at Pawsley sitting next to her, but not too close. She has a devious look in her eyes as she says, "So, Paws. Did you know you snore when you're sleeping?"

"Yeah? If I'm sleeping, how would I know that?" He's staring back at her now, knowing she's waiting for some sort of smart come-back.

Before she can answer, he says, "And by the way, did you know your tail blows up like a feather duster when you're scared?"

"Hey! I wasn't scared!" Catchoo says defensively. "I just wanted you to see that light moving around downstairs."

It looks like everything is back to normal. Catchoo is back to being Catchoo as she continues. "And did you also know Pawsley, that you drool when you snarl?" She rolls over on the bed and laughs.

"Oh yeah? Well, I'm telling you, Catchoo. If you *ever* bite my ear again, I'll show you what a *real* snarl is all about!" He teasingly bares his teeth at her.

We hear Lucy and her parents coming upstairs to go back to bed.

"G'night Mom. G'night Daddy."

"G'night Honey." Her dad hugs her as he goes off to bed.

Her mom follows Lucy into our room to tuck her in and says, "You okay now? It's really late, so I hope you can go right back to sleep."

"Yep. I'm fine. I'll have my protector right here beside me all night."

She slips under the covers as Catchoo jumps down. Pawsley is still sitting on the foot of the bed. Her mom kisses Lucy goodnight and says, "Sleep tight Honey. I love you. Good thing tomorrow is Saturday. You can sleep as late as you want."

"'night Mom. I love you too."

Her mom turns, ruffles Pawsley's ears affectionately and says, "G'night Pawsley. You keep my little girl safe, okay? You're a good dog!"

After her mom leaves, Lucy sits up and says, "What a good boy you are, Pawsley. Who knew you were such a fearless watchdog! I love you!"

Lucy gives him a hug, lays back down and says goodnight to all of us.

"I love you too Catchoo. And I love you too Pookie, and it's a good thing you were safe in your house. Hope all Pawsley's barking didn't scare you."

We all look at her, then give each other knowing looks.

Lucy turns out the light and goes to sleep.

Catchoo goes over to her own bed.

Pawsley sighs. He turns around and round and round in a circle on Lucy's bed till he finds the perfect spot to lay down.

Me? I'm wide awake.

What a crazy and exciting night, I think to myself. I'm happy everyone is safe. Happy that my friends recognize that just because I'm small, doesn't mean I'm not an important part of this family team.

And we are a team.

They told me that if it weren't for me, the *prowler* probably would have become an *intruder.*

I'm humbled.

And yet filled with pride.

I shake my head, still in disbelief at all that's happened.

I still have a small stash of peeled sunflower seeds that I'd been saving for my trips out at night.

I have them hidden in a corner under a pile of fluff. Everything turned out okay, so I reward myself by eating a few.

Since I couldn't complete my mission tonight, I jump into my wheel to get some exercise.

I run like crazy!

Fast!

I feel the wind blowing through my whiskers and over my ears, flattening them to my head.

Closing my eyes, it's easy to imagine I'm running free.

My wheel turns silently.

The longer I run, the more speed I gain. It seems I'm going faster than I did when I won the race at the pet store.

Effortless.

In my mind, I *am* running free ... free in a field of sunflowers.

Eating all the seeds I want!

And it makes me smile.

A MESSAGE FROM POOKIE

You all know by now how much I love sunflower seeds. But I know I'm not supposed to eat a lot all at once. They're supposed to be *treats*. But did you know there are other treats I like? And also allowed to eat?

Dried pumpkin seeds! Yum! And squash seeds. And I like peanuts too. NO salt, of course. It's fun to chew on the shells to get to the nut inside. Lucy gives me the small ones that only have ONE nut.

It's a good thing for me to chew on things to keep my teeth in good shape.

I also like certain veggies. Lucy gives me a small piece of broccoli, cucumber or zucchini sometimes. When I'm done eating, she takes any leftovers out of my dish right away.

Vegies are refreshing. And good for me.

And I like bits of hard-boiled egg or tofu. But Lucy makes sure I don't get too much.

She knows it's important for me to eat my hamster food. The solid block kind. It's good for my teeth to chew on them, and they taste good!

I'm NOT supposed to have sugar or salt. You can email me if you have questions about other foods it's okay for me to eat. Or about foods I should NOT eat.

Like almonds. I will *never* eat an almond! I know it could make me *very very* sick!

You can email me at:

HamstersTales@gmail.com

When you email me, I can also let you know when my next book will be available! And I will never share your name or information with anyone else!

I'd also like to know what you think about *this* book. It helps me to continue my stories when you write a review on Amazon.

Thank you for reading about my adventures!

Your friend,

Pookie

Made in the USA
Monee, IL
03 December 2019

17860874R00074